PUFFIN BOOKS

FANNY WITCH AN

Jeremy Strong once work
three thousand doughnut
stories instead, which he
of three he fell out of a fir
on his head. His mother says that this damaged him for the
of his life and refuses to take any responsibility. He loves
writing stories because he says it is 'the only time you alone
have complete control and can make anything happen.' His
ambition is to make you laugh (or at least snuffle). Jeremy
Strong lives in Kent with his family, which includes a small but
very noticeable cat called Machiavelli.

Fanny Witch and the Wicked Wizard

Jeremy Strong

Illustrated by Annabel Spenceley

PUFFIN BOOKS

PUFFIN BOOKS

Published by the Penguin Group
Penguin Books Ltd, 27 Wrights Lane, London W8 5TZ, England
Penguin Books USA Inc., 375 Hudson Street, New York, New York 10014, USA
Penguin Books Australia Ltd, Ringwood, Victoria, Australia
Penguin Books Canada Ltd, 10 Alcorn Avenue, Toronto, Ontario, Canada M4V 3B2
Penguin Books (NZ) Ltd, 182–190 Wairau Road, Auckland 10, New Zealand

Penguin Books Ltd, Registered Offices: Harmondsworth, Middlesex, England

First published as *Fanny Witch Goes Spikky-Spoo!* in Puffin Books 1992
Reissued as *Fanny Witch and the Wicked Wizard* 1995
10 9 8 7 6 5 4 3 2 1

Text copyright © Jeremy Strong, 1992
Illustrations copyright © Annabel Spenceley, 1992
All rights reserved

The moral right of the author has been asserted

Filmset in Monophoto Bembo

Printed in England by Clays Ltd, St Ives plc

Contents

Fanny Witch
and the
Safari Park

This is Fanny Witch. She is small and round and has a nose like a potato – quite a big one too. Her hat is very bent because she wears it in bed. Her black dress looks one hundred years old and has never been ironed. It has forty-two patches.

Here is Casserole the dog. He is rather old, rather hairy and just a bit smelly, but Fanny loves him very much.

This is the tumbledown cottage
next to the school, where Fanny
Witch and Casserole live. The roof
leaks. The windows are falling out.
Fanny doesn't mind because the
cottage is used by lots of animals
who have made their homes inside.

There are mice and badgers and
rabbits and owls and foxes and
spiders and beetles and robins and
hedgehogs and moths and . . . well,
LOTS.

Here is Fanny's handbag. Inside she
has got one magic fork (her wand
was chewed up by Casserole), three
hamsters, half a bar of chocolate, two
sugar cubes (in case she meets a
hungry horse) and a pair of
spectacles about which she has
forgotten.

Fanny Witch is the only teacher in
the little village school and the
children have very odd lessons.
Sometimes they do Adding Up.

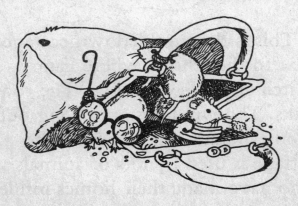

Sometimes they find out about The
Romans. But most of the time they
do Spelling. This is their best subject,
and it is not like the spelling you do.
When the village children do
Spelling, Fanny teaches them spells.
(But only nice, simple ones, like how
to turn a mud pie into a sausage roll.)

Sometimes the parents get cross
about this. They think Adding Up
and The Romans are VERY
IMPORTANT. But when they run

out of food and the shops are shut one of the children will say: 'Don't worry, I'll get some mud!' A moment later everyone has sausage rolls to eat. Then the parents can see that Spelling – the Fanny Witch Method – is useful after all.

The children love going to school. It is such a lively place. When Daniel opens his desk he is more likely to find a squirrel than a book. Amy cannot use her bag at all because there is a robin nesting in it.

'This place is like a zoo,' said Jessica one morning.

'It isn't,' said Max, who likes arguing. 'Most of the animals are

missing. In a real zoo there are lions
and tigers and elephants and
everything. We've only got foxes and
stuff.'

Casserole gave a low growl. He
didn't like being called 'stuff'. Fanny
Witch thought for a moment. 'Well,
I will tell you what we could do. If
you find some pictures of animals
and cut them out I shall make a
spell.'

Sarah's eyes popped. 'Will they
come alive?' she asked.

'But of course,' answered Fanny.
'But don't worry. We shall be quite

safe in the classroom. We'll let them wander round the playground for a bit. Then I shall undo the spell.'

There was great excitement. Max said it would be like having their own safari park. They soon found some pictures. There were baboons and lions and hippos and a giraffe. The children put the pictures out on the playground, and Fanny told everyone to go inside.

Fanny searched her handbag and

pulled out her spectacles. 'Ikky spikky spoo!' she cried, waving her spectacles at the pictures. 'Oh. Oh dear. My magic fork doesn't work any more. What a pity.'

One of the children ran out and got Fanny's magic fork from the handbag and took the spectacles from her. 'Oh!' cried Fanny. 'Silly me! I ought to wear glasses! Now, ikky spikky spoo!'

There was a bright flash. Fanny grabbed at her hat and hurried to the classroom. As the smoke cleared

the children gasped. There in the
playground were two lions, eight
baboons, three hippos and a very tall
giraffe.

The baboons made straight for the
swings and the climbing-frame, where
they jumped up and down madly.
The three hippos looked slowly round
the playground as if to say, *Now
how on earth did we get* here? The
lions padded around in silence.
(Casserole was trying to hide in
Fanny's big handbag. He didn't seem

to know that half his bottom and all his waggy tail were sticking out.)

'This is like being in Africa,' murmured Jenny. 'Now we really have got a safari park. It's just like the real thing.'

'Yes,' said Max, grinning with delight. 'It is just like the real thing except that the animals are escaping!'

There was a rush to the window and Max pointed to the fence at the back of the playground. As they watched, the giraffe delicately

stepped over the fence and wandered
off towards the village. Fanny's face
fell. 'Oh no! I must go and get it
back.' She ran out into the
playground.

The lions, baboons and hippos
were surprised to see a dumpy black
figure flapping towards them. The
lions roared and showed their teeth,
which looked rather sharp to Fanny
Witch, so she shouted back at them.
'Shoo! Go away! I've no time for

20

your nonsense. I've got a giraffe to catch!'

The baboons howled and jumped straight over the fence, closely followed by the two lions. As for the hippos, perhaps they felt lonely now. They were no good at jumping fences, so they simply crashed straight through. KERRINCH! KERRUNCH!

Fanny Witch clutched her head and wailed, 'Oh dear! Whatever shall I do now?' She hurried down to the village, with all the children following not far behind. Some way behind them came Casserole, creeping along and growling to himself because it helped him feel braver. However, he was not brave enough to open his eyes and he walked right into a big cardboard box someone had left on the road. It fell over him and a struggle began as he tried to escape.

There was big trouble in the

village. Daniel's mother was trying to stop the baboons ripping up all her washing. Then there was a sudden scream from Jessica's house. Her father came running out into the street wrapped in a big towel. 'A giraffe just poked its head into my bathroom!' he stuttered. 'And I was having a bath!'

'The hippos are having a bath too,' said Max, who was secretly enjoying all this. Max was right. The three hippos had plodded down to the village pond. Now they lay there snorting and blowing bubbles at the village ducks.

Fanny Witch was getting worried. She could see the giraffe munching a pair of bathroom curtains. She could

see the hippos in the pond. She
counted all eight baboons still playing
tug o'war with the washing. But
where were the two lions? If only
she could get all the animals back
together she could make an undoing
spell and turn them back into
pictures. Where *were* the two lions?

All at once there was a huge roar
from the end of the street and the
lions came charging towards the
children. 'Quick! Run for cover!'
cried Fanny. She grabbed the
chocolate from her handbag and

waved it fiercely at the lions. 'Ikky
spikky bother, where's my fork?'

The children screamed and then,
suddenly, the lions had gone. They
had raced right past them. They
were scared stiff too, and roaring
with terror. Behind them came a
terrible monster, unlike any beast
anyone had seen before. In fact, it
looked like a cardboard box on legs
and it was making growly noises.

Fanny Witch seized her moment.
'Ikky spikky spoo!' she cried, this time
actually waving the magic fork. In a
flash the giraffe, the hippos, the lions
and baboons had all vanished. All
that was left were some coloured

pictures, floating in the air. Fanny grabbed them and put them safely in her handbag.

'Phew, that was close,' she murmured. Just then the cardboard box crashed into her legs and gave a startled yelp. 'Now what strange thing have we here?' asked Fanny, lifting up the box. 'Casserole! It was you! You saved us from the animals – you are brave!'

Casserole barked and barked and barked to prove how very brave he was. He licked Fanny's chin and her nose and her neck and her ears and . . . 'You can stop now,' said Fanny. 'I think that is enough of a wash for one day.'

Max looked up at Fanny. 'Can we have another safari park tomorrow? It was brilliant.'

'I don't think so, Max. Perhaps we shall have a quiet day tomorrow.'

Jessica's father rolled his eyes and muttered to himself, 'A quiet day? Fat chance there is of that happening with Fanny Witch around! I'm going to finish my bath.'

Fanny Witch
and the
Cloud-beast

Fanny Witch was feeling very pleased
with herself. She had been getting fed
up with the long walk to the village
shop. It was even worse coming
back, loaded down with shopping.
But now she thought she had solved
the problem. Fanny had bought a
donkey. His name was Solomon.

'Now I can ride into the village,'
she told Casserole, 'and Solomon can
carry all my shopping back for me.

Won't that be a good idea?' Casserole took one look at the donkey then ran away and hid under the bed covers. He thought he had never seen such a big dog.

As for Solomon, he carried on eating the roses round the back door.

Fanny Witch tied some rope round Solomon's neck. She fetched a chair, stood on it and climbed on to his back.

'Come on, Solomon, off we go.' Solomon chewed a pink rose. 'Come on, gee-up!' Fanny tugged at the rope. Solomon tugged back and carried on eating. 'Oh, do come on!'

Fanny tapped his sides with her feet. Solomon lifted his grey head and brayed loudly. Then he lowered his head. Lower and lower went his head until his neck was stretched out like a hairy slide. 'Oh-wo-wo-wo-wo-oh!' went Fanny Witch and FLUMP! She slid right down Solomon's neck and into the cabbage patch.

'You are a lot of use, I must say!' grumbled Fanny, looking for her hat, which had come off in the fall. Solomon was slowly chewing it with his huge yellow teeth. Fanny snatched it back. 'I suppose you think my hat is a giant black carrot? Well, you can think again. I'm going to the shop.'

The sun was shining brightly, so Fanny was surprised to find the village covered by a large cloud. It was sitting on top of the village looking very dark and cross. It was no ordinary cloud at all, but a very damp and thick cloud. It made everything in the village wet. Carpets went squelchy, curtains went limp and wallpaper began to peel. Inside their houses the villagers were full of coughs and chills, aches and pains.

'Oh dear,' murmured Fanny. 'Unless I am very much mistaken that looks like a Cloud-beast. How very nasty.' Casserole crawled under Fanny's dress. 'There is no need for that,' said Fanny. 'We are quite safe, but I am afraid the village is in great danger. Everyone will soon be shivering to death. I must do something.'

Fanny went straight back to the house and got out her Big Book of Spells. The bit about the Cloud-beast did not make nice reading and Fanny was glad when she had finished. She went out into the sunny garden,

because reading about the Cloud-beast had made *her* shiver. She sat down on the old bench and tried to think of a plan. She thought very, very hard, so quite soon she was fast asleep.

She was woken by Solomon. He was slowly munching the end of her hat. Fanny snatched it back. 'You useless old lump,' said Fanny severely. 'What am I going to do about the Cloud-beast? If I want to attack it I shall need to dodge about quickly, or it will blast me with lightning, or something worse.'

Fanny gazed at the old donkey and a sparkle came to her eye. 'I know how to deal with that grumpy old Cloud-beast!' She grabbed her handbag and pulled out the magic fork. 'Ikky spikky spoo!' There was a flash and a startled bray from Solomon. As the pink smoke cleared it showed a new Solomon, an improved Solomon. He had grown wings – great big beautiful wings.

Casserole ran round and round, barking. He wanted wings too. Solomon lifted his head proudly and bellowed. 'Now – giddy-up!' cried Fanny, leaping on to the donkey's back. 'And I mean UP!'

With one leap Solomon was in the air, his powerful wings beating steadily. 'You're a wonder, Solomon, a marvel!' shouted Fanny. 'Let's show that Cloud-beast a thing or two.' They plunged down and galloped right along the great grey humped back of the Cloud-beast. KER-LUMP, KER-LUMP, KER-LUMP!

The Cloud-beast growled and heaved. 'Hey, what's going on?' It looked all round, but saw nothing. Down swooped Fanny and Solomon again. KER-LUMP, KER-LUMP, KER-LUMP! 'Ow! Stop it!' The Cloud-beast rolled its eyes and out of one corner spotted the donkey as he climbed into the sky once more.

'So that's your game, is it? Take that!' The Cloud-beast spurted millions of giant hail-stones into the sky. The startled donkey wildly pawed the air and Fanny almost fell right off. Her legs waved about madly, showing all the stripes on her stripy stockings. (You could see her blue knickers too!) Fanny clung to Solomon's neck.

'Climb higher,' she cried, and the

donkey struggled upwards, out of reach of the icy hail-stones. 'Now listen, Solomon, you will be quite safe with me. Come on, now, down we go.'

Again the Cloud-beast blasted out hail-stones, but Fanny pointed the magic fork and, 'Ikky spikky spoo!' the hail-stones turned into a fluttering cloud of butterflies. Down went Fanny and Solomon and KER-LUMP, KER-LUMP, KER-LUMP!

'Owee zowee! Stop that at once!' yelled the furious Cloud-beast. 'I'll get you!' The Cloud-beast wound itself round and round. His grey body grew darker. All at once a Cloud-snake raised its poisonous head. There was a flash and a shaft of lightning arrowed past Fanny. Solomon kicked his heels and galloped across the sky.

'I don't like this,' muttered Fanny, as another blast of lightning set the tip of her hat on fire. 'Let's see if that Cloud-snake likes his own medicine.' Fanny waved her fork. A moment later she held up a round, shining mirror, just like a shield.

The Cloud-snake fired more lightning bolts. Fanny steadied Solomon and held up the mirror-shield. The lightning struck the centre, bounced off in a shower of sparks, and went hurtling back at the Cloud-snake. It pierced the monster's tail like a giant wasp sting.

The Cloud-snake leaped up with a wild cry, then crashed down. He lay moaning and groaning and thrashing

his throbbing tail. Down came Fanny
and Solomon – KER-LUMP,
KER-LUMP, KER-LUMP!

'Stop it, stop it!' cried the Cloud-
beast.

'Go away then,' shouted Fanny.
'And don't ever come back.'

But the Cloud-beast refused to go
and fired off another shaft of
lightning. It bounced off Fanny's
shield, came flashing back and buried
itself in the Cloud-beast's bottom.
'Yikey-yikey-yoooh!' screeched the
monster. With a great groan the
Cloud-beast crawled away, throwing

out snow and rain, sleet and hail and little flashes of lightning. Away it went, over the hill, until it disappeared for ever.

Solomon glided down to the village. 'You were magnificent,' said Fanny. The big donkey poked out his tongue and licked Fanny's big nose. Out came the villagers, sneezing from all the damp, but very happy. The children wanted rides on Solomon, of course. He had to go up and fly round the village over and over again before they were all satisfied, but he was very good about it.

When at last they got back to the school house, Fanny performed a little spell with her magic fork and Solomon found himself wingless once more. He was not at all pleased about *that*, and stood for ages with his head buried deep in a big elderberry bush, sulking.

'Never mind,' said Fanny. 'You

have been very brave and I am proud
of you.' To show just how proud
she was, Fanny got her second-best
hat and waved it in front of the
donkey. Solomon's ears pricked up.
He pulled his big head out of the
bush and nudged the hat several
times.

'Oh, I see. I know what you
want.' Fanny cut two holes in the
brim and pulled the hat down on
Solomon's head. He snorted with
pleasure and marched round the
garden six times to show everyone.
Then he settled down by the back
door and began to steadily chew the
roses. The pink ones were truly
delicious.

*Fanny Witch
and the
Washing-machine*

Fanny Witch woke up one morning
feeling hungry. 'Time for supper,'
she said to Casserole. (Fanny always
got her mealtimes muddled up – and
the days muddled – *and* the months!)
She went to the kitchen cupboard. It
was empty, except for two barn-
owls that had made their home
inside. 'Oh,' said Fanny. 'Ooooooh,'
said the barn-owls.

'I do beg your pardon,' said
Fanny, and shut the cupboard door.

'I had better go to the shops.' Fanny took her purse and set off for the village with Casserole at her heels. (He liked to grab the hem of her skirt and take *her* for a walk.)

When they got to the shop Fanny filled her basket with food. She got her purse, opened it up and found that was just as empty as her cupboard. There was nothing inside except a large spider who waved at Fanny with a very friendly set of legs.

'Oh, I've no money left,' Fanny said to Casserole. 'I must put all these things back. Now what shall we do?'

Poor Fanny had a problem. The school was closed for the summer holiday. She could not earn any money there. She stood outside the shop and read the notices in the window. She was quite excited to see one that said:

HOME HELP WANTED TO CLEAN COOK AND WASH. GOOD PAY. PLEASE APPLY TO MRS. WHITE.

That must be Stephen and Jenny's mother, thought Fanny. *That will do me nicely. I'm very good at cleaning and tidying.* She went straight off and knocked at Mrs White's door.

It was a big house. And what was more, *children* lived in the big house, so you can imagine how untidy it was, and how much washing there was to be done.

'Thank heavens you have come,' cried Mrs White, pulling Fanny inside. 'There is so much to do I don't know where to start. It's awful, and the children never help.'

Jenny and Stephen were very pleased to see Fanny Witch. They stared hard at her big black handbag

and wondered if the magic fork was inside. They introduced Fanny to their baby sister Emma, who was one year old. Fanny lifted Emma up and gave her a cuddle. She wrinkled her potato nose.

'Hmmm, doesn't she smell a bit funny?'

'She needs a clean nappy,' Jenny said.

'She always needs clean nappies,' Stephen moaned.

'Clean nappy? No problem!' Fanny put Emma on the table and looked for her magic fork. 'Ikky spikky spoo!' The air was filled with

tiny sparkles and there was a faint
SHLURRP noise. Emma had a
fresh clean nappy. The room smelled
of roses.

'How wonderful!' laughed Mrs
White. 'I wish I could do that. But
can you clean the whole house with
a spell?'

Fanny Witch thought carefully. 'I
know a washing spell and a cleaning
spell. If I put them together and add
a bit extra, because it's a big house,
it should work very well.'

They went into the front garden.
Casserole seemed to know what to
expect and hid himself under a bush.
Fanny jabbed the air with her fork
and shouted, 'Ikky spikky spoo!'
There was a loud BANG! The air
was filled with a throbbing noise, like
some giant machine at work.

'What's happening?' whispered
Mrs White, as the ground beneath
her feet began to tremble.

'Look!' shouted Stephen. 'The
house is filling up with water!'

Mrs White grabbed Fanny's arm.
'Are you sure this is all right?'

'Don't worry,' said Fanny. 'I have made a —'

Her words were drowned by a deep gurgle. The house walls shook. Great frothy bubbles could be seen through the windows. The water whirled and twirled, faster and faster. Tables and chairs, sofas and beds, cupboards and books and toys began to whiz round and round.

BAMMA BAMMA SQUOODGE
SQUIDGE, BAMMA BAMMA
SQUOODGE SQUIDGE went
the whole house. Fanny Witch had
turned it into a gigantic washing-
machine.

Mrs White and the children were
horrified. Words stuck in their
throats. Casserole was now digging a
hole under the bush so he could
crawl into it. But Fanny Witch
looked pleased.

'I think my spell is working well, don't you?' Bubbles were beginning to pop up from the chimney and float away. At last Jenny found her voice.

'But everything will get broken,' she squeaked.

'My bed has gone round four times already,' said Stephen, who looked as if his eyes had gone round four times too.

Fanny frowned and stumped up to the house. She peered through a window. A sofa went swishing past her eyes in a swirl of froth. It was closely followed by Stephen's bed

(for the fifth time), and all Jenny's clothes. Bubbles were pouring thick and fast from the chimney. Fanny began to wonder if she had put too much soap powder into her spell.

Suddenly one of the upstairs windows broke with a mighty crash. A river of soapy water came gushing out. With the water came a table, eighty-five books, seven mixed pairs of shoes, thirteen dresses, Emma's cot,

three armchairs, most of the
saucepans, a bicycle and the
grandfather clock. And still it went on.
BAMMA BAMMA SQUOODGE
SQUIDGE, BAMMA BAMMA
SQUOODGE SQUIDGE.

'Stop the spell, please!' cried Jenny,
tugging at Fanny's sleeve.

Even Fanny Witch was beginning
to think that maybe her spell was a
bit out of hand. She waved her
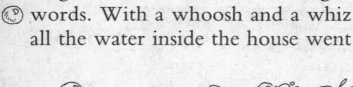
magic fork and shouted the magic
words. With a whoosh and a whiz
all the water inside the house went

shooting up the chimney. It sprayed
out over the village like a giant
foaming fountain. (In fact, quite a lot
of people got a surprise bubble bath.)

The house had stopped throbbing.
A thin trickle of water came from
under the front door. Mrs White
tried to open it. The way was
blocked by a bedroom cupboard.
Even so, Mrs White could see that
the place was now a soggy mess.
Fanny Witch smiled cheerfully.

'It all looks nice and sparkly clean,'
she said brightly.

'But it's soaking,' wailed Mrs
White.

'I could do a spin-dry spell,' said
Fanny helpfully. 'That would soon
get it dry.'

Mrs White began to push Fanny
down the garden path. 'No, thank
you, Fanny Witch. Just leave us alone.
Thank you for your help, but no
more spells – please! Just go home!'

Fanny went back to her tumbledown cottage. 'Some people are very odd, Casserole,' she said. 'When you offer help they just don't want to know. Oh well, I had better magic us some breakfast.'

Casserole began to bark. He was always happy to see any food, any time, anywhere.

A few days later Fanny met Mrs White in the village, and she asked how the housework was going. Mrs White frowned. 'It is rather odd. Jenny and Stephen never used to help at all, but now they tidy their rooms every day and I don't need any extra help. I've even taken that notice out of the shop window.'

Fanny was happy to hear this, but she was puzzled too. Jenny explained everything when she saw Fanny one afternoon. 'We still don't like housework, but we would rather do housework than have the whole house turned into a giant washing-machine again. The armchairs are still a bit squelchy to sit on!'

Stephen gave Fanny a big smile. 'The bubble bit was brilliant. If you like you can turn my bedroom into a washing-machine.' Casserole started barking loudly. He grabbed Fanny's dress and began to pull her down the street and back home. There was no way he was going to let Fanny do any more washing spells.

Fanny Witch
and the
Wicked Wizard

One day a stranger came to the little
village. He was very old and walked
in a slow shuffle. He wore thin gold
glasses, and behind these glasses were
a pair of small, very black eyes. As
soon as anyone looked at those eyes
and found them staring back they
would quickly turn away, as if they
had seen something very frightening.

The children noticed it most of all
and they would not go near the old

man. Their parents thought this was
a bit rude.

'There's nothing wrong with
Doctor Blackliver,' said Daniel's
mother. 'He won't bite you. He's
only an old man.' All the same,
Daniel was scared when he saw those
beady eyes. He ran away, like
everyone else.

One morning Doctor Blackliver
appeared outside the school
playground. He stood there watching
the children running about and
laughing, until he was spotted by
Sarah. She pointed the old man out
to Fanny Witch.

'So that is who I have been
hearing so much about,' said Fanny.
She went over to introduce herself.

'Oh, I know who you are,' snapped
Doctor Blackliver. 'There is no need
to tell me. Everyone knows about the
famous Fanny Witch and how kind
and how nice and how clever and
. . . Bah!' The doctor eyed Fanny
through his gold-rimmed glasses.
'Well, do you want to know
something, Fanny Witch? You make
me feel ill! You make my blood boil
and my eyes pop!'

Fanny took several steps back and Casserole dashed under her big black dress to get away from this horrid old man. 'I'm sure I didn't mean to upset you . . .' began Fanny.

'No, of course you didn't. *You* wouldn't dream of upsetting anyone,' sneered Doctor Blackliver. 'I hate you, Fanny Witch. I hate the way you make everyone happy. I hate the

way you manage to stay young at heart, and most of all I HATE CHILDREN!' The doctor spat out the last words as if they were something that tasted horrible.

Fanny was getting angry. She did not see why a cross old man should come to the school just to be rude. Fanny Witch was also getting danger signals. There was something strange about the old man. A shiver of fear ran up and down her spine. 'I think you had better go home, Doctor Blackliver, before you upset the children,' said Fanny. 'I don't understand why you want to be so nasty.'

All the crossness vanished from the doctor's face and a big smile appeared. 'I thought I would take one last look at them all before . . .' He stopped and smiled again. Fanny felt a cold chill in her heart.

'Before what?' she asked.

But Doctor Blackliver had turned away and was shuffling back down the street, cackling to himself. Fanny felt a hot little hand pushed into hers. It was Ellie.

'He's a horrible man,' she whispered. 'You must be careful, Fanny Witch.'

'Yes, Ellie. I think you are right. We must all be careful.'

The very next morning Fanny was woken by a loud hammering on her front door.

'Fanny! Fanny Witch! Come down at once, it's terrible! What are we going to do?'

Standing at the door were many villagers. Some of them had tears streaming down their faces. 'Whatever is the matter?' asked Fanny. She had never seen the villagers so upset before.

'It's our children, our lovely children,' wailed Stephen's mother. 'Come and see for yourself.'

The villagers tugged at Fanny's cloak and almost pulled her out of the little cottage and down the road to the village. At last they reached one of the houses and went in. 'Come and see,' whispered Jessica's mother, almost beside herself. She called up the stairs. 'Jessica, come and show Fanny Witch what has happened.'

There was a rustle from upstairs and a croaky voice called out, 'What? Who's that? Speak up now.' There were shambling footsteps on the wooden stairs and Jessica appeared. Fanny could not recognize her. She stared as a hunched little old lady came stumbling down the stairs. Her face was covered with deep wrinkles. Her hair was thin and grey.

'Jessica?' said Fanny softly. 'Is that really you?' The little old woman nodded and her eyes filled with tears. 'But how did . . .' Fanny began.

'The other village children are the same,' muttered Mr Shaw.

'Ellie and Daniel, Sarah, Stephen, Max, every single one. Oh, Fanny,

what has happened to them? What
are we going to do? There must be
something you can do!'

Fanny Witch shook her head and
sat down heavily in a chair. 'I should
have known,' she kept saying. 'I
should have known. I could feel it in
my bones. I knew there was
something wrong.'

The villagers crowded round her.
'Tell us. It can't be any worse than

what has already happened.'

Fanny Witch looked up at the desperate faces all round her. She took a deep breath. 'It is Doctor Blackliver. He is a wizard. I should have known straight away. I felt the warnings, but I never expected a wizard to come to our little village. Why should he?'

'Can anything be done?' asked Max's mother.

'There are many kinds of witch and wizard,' said Fanny. 'Doctor Blackliver is one of the very worst kind. He cannot bear to see happiness, so he tries to make as many people as unhappy as possible. Even worse, he cannot bear to see young people, because he is old and wrinkled himself. He doesn't understand that it is how your heart feels that makes you young or old.'

'But can anything be done?' repeated Max's mother.

Fanny Witch got up. 'I shall have to think. You must understand that because Doctor Blackliver is a wizard he cannot harm me, but his magic is stronger than mine. I shall have to think of a different way to tackle this problem. Magic will not be much use this time.'

Fanny walked back through the village. At each house she saw an ancient child. Little Ellie had to use two walking-sticks to come hobbling down the path. Max had a wispy beard and was bent double. Sarah's hair had fallen out.

Fanny was heart-broken. She shut

herself in the little tumbledown cottage where nobody could see and cried. Casserole sat at her feet, screwed up his eyes and howled. 'How can anyone be so heartless?' sniffed Fanny. 'And what can we do about it, Casserole? How can we possibly make it all better?'

She got out her Big Book of Spells and turned the dusty pages. Five times she read through the book and then shut it with a bang. 'That's no

good at all! There's nothing, *nothing* I can do to help those children. I feel as helpless as a baby!'

Casserole gave a loud bark and Fanny stopped in her tracks. 'What did I just say, Casserole — as helpless as a baby, eh? Maybe babies aren't so helpless after all. I have got a tiny idea that might just work.'

Fanny whizzed back through the Big Book of Spells. 'Ah, a little magic trick for myself! Ikky spikky spoo!'

There was a loud gurgling and a puff of green smoke. Fanny had vanished. Sitting in her place was a little baby, just one year old. The baby pushed open the front door and

crawled off down the path. Casserole, who was getting used to Fanny's strange ways, followed at a safe distance. (In other words he kept well out of sight.)

Down the road went the little baby, gurgling to herself. Suddenly a black shadow fell across her. She stopped, sat back and looked up. An old man with thin gold glasses gazed down at her. His mouth was set in a crooked smile.

'Well, well, well,' said Doctor Blackliver. 'What have we here? You must be the last one, and the youngest too.'

'Goo, goo, goo,' said the baby.

'I'm going to give you a present,' hissed the wizard. 'Since you are the youngest person in this village I am going to turn you into the oldest. I am going to make you one hundred and one years old. Your hair will fall out. Your teeth will fall out. Your bones will creak.'

'Goo, goo, goo – oops,' went the baby, as a small puddle appeared just where she was sitting.

Doctor Blackliver looked at the baby in disgust and pulled a long wand from his sleeve. He waved it in huge zigzags over the baby's head. 'Nakky noo nah!' he cried. Nothing happened. Not a thing. 'Nakky noo nah!' yelled Doctor Blackliver. The baby smiled up at the purple-faced wizard.

'Nakky noo goo goo,' she giggled.

'Nakky noo nah!' screamed Doctor Blackliver for the third time. He began to jump up and down in his rage. He yelled at Fanny and waved his wand so hard it broke.

'Aargh!' screeched the doctor. He danced round and round stamping his feet. He threw himself to the ground, kicked his legs in the air and howled. His face was screwed up into a tight black rage. His big purple tongue crashed about in his mouth like a rattlesnake's death clatter. Smoke began to pour from him. All at once there was a huge BANG! Doctor Blackliver vanished altogether.

The little baby blinked and looked all round to make sure he really was gone. 'Goo, goo, ikky spikky spoo!' Fanny Witch was back to her old self, but sitting in a rather damp patch. Fanny hastily got up.

From every house in the village there were cries of wonder. The children came running out, their parents with them. Fanny had never seen so many smiles and tears of joy. When Doctor Blackliver had gone, so had all the signs of old age. Everyone crowded round Fanny, patting her on the back and thanking her, while Casserole danced round and round them all.

'How did you do it?' they asked.

'Simple. Doctor Blackliver got so cross that he overheated and exploded,' said Fanny. 'I knew he couldn't harm me because I am a witch after all. I changed myself into a little baby and when he couldn't turn me into an old crone he had the biggest temper tantrum of all time and, well, you know the rest.'

Fanny was lifted from her feet and was carried round the village. 'Three cheers for Fanny Witch!' cried the villagers. 'Hip, hip, hooray! Hip, hip, hooray! Hip, hip –'

'Woof!' barked Casserole. 'Woof, woof, woof!'